D1261489

Praise for Super Socks

"This is such an endearing, insightful, special little book about the joys and struggles of having a sibling with special needs. A joy to read!"

—Cheri Glover, artist and mom of a child with autism

"Super Socks by Connie Bowman illustrates how special children and adults with special needs are. The pure imagination and attention to small details is refreshing and different. We are all different, but for those who seem to be a little more different than expected, it is often a difficult journey. This is a wonderful exploration of the importance of patience and true understanding, and of the rich and comforting internal worlds of special needs children. Thanks, Connie."

—Kevin Collabucci, Special Olympics coach and parent of a special needs child

"What a great book! Not only is it fun for kids, but it is a great go-to book to help parents begin the conversation about the acceptance of differences!"

—Alison Mitzner, MD, pediatrician, family wellness expert, fitness advocate, writer, media contributor, and mom of two

"It seems to me that something magical happens when we embrace diversity and celebrate the fact that everyone's voice has something of value to share in the circle of learning. This book creatively reminds us that we become better people when we accept and learn from the uniqueness of others."

—Sue Leader Miller, theater educator

"Doing things differently or being a little different certainly keeps life interesting. In *Super Socks,* two sisters experience how their differences help inspire and empower others to appreciate diversity. Three-year-old Katie, who has Down syndrome, chooses her big sister's socks each day. Her mismatched choices help her sister to understand there is beauty in the many contrasts of life. *Super Socks* is a short story that presents a valuable life lesson for not only children, but people of all ages."

—Cynthia Parr, executive director, ARC of Howard County, MD

More praise for Super Socks

"I love this book, and I love the blessing of having a daughter with Down syndrome. To have her in my life strips away the ridiculous and helps me focus on the beautiful and the joyful. Through her, I have found that beauty lies in simple measures, and she has given me a much better perspective and life than I could have ever imagined without her."

> —Michelle Graves, proud mother of a daughter with Down syndrome

"In *Super Socks*, Connie Bowman shows us a portrait of what it is like to live and learn with someone who has a disability. This book is wonderful for all students and will help promote awareness and the importance of acceptance."

> —Dana Beyer, teacher of students with learning disabilities.

"Why is Molly so sensitive about her socks? Like Molly, I grew up with something most people cannot understand: the emotional impact of having a sibling with a disability. Molly might appear sensitive to some, but in reality it's just her way of fighting for her sister. We become protectors first; it's our first instinct. *Super Socks* is a conversation starter that will hopefully lead to unity and acceptance in today's youth."

> —Amanda Owen, author of *Pieces of Me*

"Children are magical in their ability to accept the world as it is. Given the chance, they are brave souls. No place is that bravery more evident than among children born with Down syndrome. These children acknowledge what is, without resisting or denying, but simply accepting—with joy—all things new and different. In Connie Bowman's *Super Socks*, children will learn an enduring lesson about accepting the things that make us unique!"

> —Deborah Hawkins Wright, M.A., CAPM,
> founder of Inside/Out Loving You Life Strategies Consulting

"Like Molly and Katie, we can all choose to celebrate diversity and let our differences and our love unite us."

> —Jason Kimmel, director/instructor, children's theatre

SUPER SOCKS

story by **Connie Bowman**

illustrations by **Kelly O'Neill**

Brandylane
Publishers, Inc.
Publishing books since 1985

ISBN: 978-1-947860-73-5
LCCN: 2019909652

Designed by Michael Hardison
Project managed by Haley Simpkiss

Printed in the United States of America

Published by
Brandylane Publishers, Inc.
5 S. 1st Street
Richmond, Virginia 23219

Brandylane
Publishers, Inc.
Publishing books since 1985

brandylanepublishers.com

For Beau.

For Mabel, Loretta, Robert, Lily, and Thomas.

For all children and children at heart,

with love and gratitude for your kindness.

It's time I let you in on a *secret*.

What I'm about to share with you
WILL
change
your
life.

Only

turn

the

page

IF

you're

absolutely

ready.

Consider

yourself

WARNED!

Okay:

YOUR SOCKS HAVE
SUPER POWERS.

I'm not kidding.

My sock drawer is full to overflowing; full of super socks. They're all different. Most don't even have a match. (I'm convinced the washing machine eats them.) Which is fine for me and my little sister, Katie. She wears super socks too.

In fact, super socks were all Katie's idea.

Katie will pair a hot pink sock with an orange one.

Or a multi-color striped sock and one with puppy dogs.

It seems there's no limit to my sister's creative genius!

Katie's only three, so she's too little to have real chores yet. (Lucky!) But she still likes to help out. After dinner, she can't wait to help me with the dishes. When I feed the cat, she gives him water.

And every morning, when I'm getting ready for school, Katie picks out my socks for me. It's her most important job, and she takes it seriously. Whatever socks Katie chooses for me, I wear them. No questions asked. I'd do anything for my sister.

Katie was born with Down syndrome. That's what we call it when a person is born with an extra chromosome. Chromosomes are tiny bundles of information inside your cells that tell your body how to work. Most people have forty-six chromosomes inside each cell, but some people, like Katie, have forty-seven instead!

People all over the world have Down syndrome. They might look a little different, and they might need help with certain things. But people with Down syndrome love to learn and have fun, just like everyone else!

Katie is one of a kind. She gives the best hugs. She's funny! Her favorite color is the whole rainbow. And she loves it when we both wear our colorful, mismatched socks. We're fearless—unstoppable, really, the two of us in our super socks. They give us the courage to bravely and kindly face people who don't understand that different is awesome. Different is fun! Anyway, who says socks have to match? After all, nobody says *sisters* have to look and be exactly the same.

My teacher, Mr. Rodriguez, calls me "Funky Socks." He gets me.

My good friends understand me too. They all love Katie as much as I do. They say that she has *style*.

And then there's Billy Sanders. He's in my grade at school.

Billy sits next to me in math. We're both pretty good at fractions—even if I'm probably a little better. He's also on my soccer team. (So maybe he's scored a couple more goals this season. Whatever.)

Billy's nice enough, I guess. But sometimes he teases me about my socks. It's *no bueno*.

Most days, it's just easier to wear long pants to school. But last picture day, I wore a new jungle-patterned dress. It went great with the pair of socks Katie picked out for me. One had my favorite animal, elephants, and the other had cute baby monkeys.

When I passed Billy in the hallway, he smiled his dazzling smile and said, "Nice dress, Molly." Then his eyes shifted downward. "Going to the zoo today?"

Billy's jokes aren't very funny, but sometimes other kids laugh. He snickered as he sauntered into class. My best friend, Lonny, practically had to hold me back from slugging him. But just in the nick of time, the superpower kicked in. It started as a warm tingle in my feet, spreading up up up and filling me like a balloon. When I use my powers, it's almost like I'm floating a few inches off the ground, too full of calm to let anything bother me. (That was a close one, though!) Billy can say whatever he likes about me. I would never tell him about Katie and our super socks. That's the big problem with having superpowers: you can't tell too many people about them.

One of Katie's favorite people is our ice cream man, Sam, who drives through our neighborhood on warm evenings around sundown. I think Sam's cool, because he thinks Katie's cool. He's the only person I know who loves rainbows as much as my sister.

Whenever she hears the familiar tune of Sam's truck, Katie will holler, "Ice cream, ice cream!" And that's my cue to scoop up some change from the jar in the hall and race with her out the door. Sometimes I let her win. But sometimes she beats me fair and square.

Sam knows just what Katie likes. "Well, if it isn't Princess Katie!" he announces, bowing with a flourish as he regally presents my sister with her favorite rainbow popsicle. Katie smiles from ear to adorable ear and thanks Sam as she tugs at the corners of her skirt, giving him a fancy little curtsy. He and Katie put on their "Princess and the Popsicle" play every single time they see each other.

One pretty spring afternoon, as Sam was handing Katie her popsicle, I heard a familiar voice say, "Love your socks, Molly."

I turned around to see Billy Sanders standing right behind me, his sly smile showing off his perfect white teeth.

I felt my cheeks go red. But before I could say anything, Katie started jumping up and down, excited.

"I picked them! I picked them!"

Billy looked down at Katie's dancing-cow-and-purple-flower combo. I crossed my arms, daring him to say something mean about my sister's socks, and felt the familiar warmth begin to rise up through my body, from my feet to my head.

Sam chimed in.

"Aren't they fabulous? Katie picks them out every day. She's got so-o-o-ome style!"

Sam winked at Katie, and Katie curtsied to him one more time. I paid Sam and bolted quickly toward our house before Billy could say another word. Katie followed, happily gobbling down her popsicle.

"Take it easy, Katie; you'll get a brain freeze," I warned, shaking off the run-in with Billy. Crisis averted, and grateful for our friend Sam and our socks, we sat peacefully on the front porch, watching the orange sunset as we polished off our desserts.

The next morning, Katie put together the best combination ever. My right sock was yellow featuring chocolate milkshakes topped with fluffy whipped cream and bright red cherries. The left had grilled cheese sandwiches with french fries. It was a yummy pairing—it even made me a little hungry!

During lunch that day, Lonny asked to see my socks. She peeked under the table as I poked my feet out and cracked up so hard that she almost choked on her turkey sandwich.

We had a good, long giggle as we finished our food. Then, from right behind me, I heard someone say, "Great socks, Molly!"

I whipped around in my seat. It was Billy Sanders, holding his lunch tray, grinning down at me once again with his blue eyes twinkling. He must have seen me showing off my socks to Lonny.

Time stopped in the lunchroom. My ears got hot. I could feel my heart beat faster. I was angry and embarrassed and terrified all at once. I tried to call up my superpower, but it wasn't working.

Why wasn't it working?

Then Billy Sanders did something that surprised me. He pulled up his right pant leg and then his left. His right sock was red with teeny-tiny baby panda bears. The left had stars and planets.

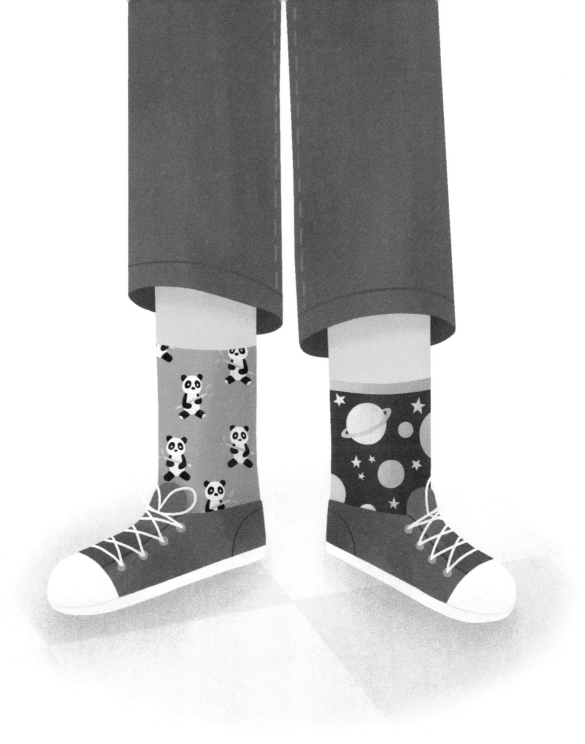

"What do you think?" Billy asked me, still smiling. I stared at his socks, and then at his face, and after a few seconds, we both busted out laughing.

It's possible I was wrong about Billy Sanders. He's actually pretty cool. He's coming over to my house this weekend to do homework with me—and to show off his super socks to Katie. We might even kick the soccer ball around.

The secret's out

about SUPER SOCKS.

And now, you know too.

About the Author

Connie Bowman is an actress and voiceover talent, as well as the author of three previous books: *Back to Happy*, *Beau's Day Care Day*, and *There's an Elephant in My Bathtub*. She lives in Maryland with her husband and chocolate lab, Sophie, and enjoys hiking, biking, cooking, running, and teaching yoga.

About the Illustrator

Kelly O'Neill loves to tell stories through cute, fun, and whimsical imagery. She earned a BFA in illustration from Syracuse University in 2017, and currently resides in Princeton, NJ, where she works creating illustrations for children's books.

CPSIA information can be obtained
at www.ICGtesting.com
Printed in the USA
LVHW071505011019
632853LV00021B/821/P

9 781947 860735